HOLDING DEMONS

IN

SMALL JARS

Holding Demons in Small Jars
Copyright © 2016 by Jasmine Kumalah
Interior and cover art copyright © 2016 by Si Jie Loo
All rights reserved.

Please respect the writer's and artist's original work. No part of this book, text or illustrations, may be reproduced without written permission. Contact the publisher at the address below.

This is a work of the imagination. Any similarity to real people or events is coincidental.

Ebook ISBN 978-0-9861516-9-9
Trade ISBN 978-0-9861516-8-2

Library of Congress Control Number: 2015959846

Book design by Frogtown Bookmaker,
frogtownbookmaker.com

Published by Lystra Books & Literary Services, LLC
391 Lystra Estates Drive, Chapel Hill, NC 27517
919-968-7877
lystrabooks@gmail.com
www.lystrabooks.com

LYSTRA BOOKS
& Literary Services

*Dedicated to the wounds in all of us
crying out to be healed.*
~ Jasmine

*To my family and loving husband Kevin.
With special gratitude to Jasmine
for entrusting me to illustrate your beautiful poetry.
And, to the memory of Michael and Kathu.
Your passions for life shall live on in my heart.*
~ Si Jie

Holding Demons in Small Jars

by
Jasmine Kumalah

illustrated by
Si Jie Loo

LYSTRA BOOKS
& Literary Services
Chapel Hill, NC

There is a war inside that slips outside,
the sort of war that leaves
men in death's embrace,
body parts asunder.
The sort of war that leaves
fears frozen and shivers trapped.

Chapter One

Detective Alu cursed the suicidal okada driver,
threw vibrant insults at the man, to no avail.
Alu hated the small okada bikes.
His tall and lanky body,
too long for the small whirring machine,
perched uncomfortably behind the driver.

But this was the quickest way
to pass through the bustling streets of Diamante,
into the edge of the city where
the bay loomed.
The bay, a gluttonous vulture,
Lingered,
filled with the bodies

of the forgotten.
Alive and the dead.
Just an hour before, Alu had received a call from his boss,
Police Chief Bergain Maxine.

There had been a murder in the bay.

A gruesome affair.

The whir of the okada
drowned the sounds of the
bustling city and Alu's curses.
His body tensed at each turn,
ready for the moment
when it
would slip and
scrape the moving ground.

A sharp turn
Left, a hapless banana seller
bristling in anger
in a cloud of
smog.

Another daring turn left, the detective
hanging a little too close to the open gutters.

Splash!

A suspicious murky
liquid sprayed
from a disturbed puddle
onto his ironed khakis.

Jasmine Kumalah

They sped through the city of Diamante,
past the new town alongside the decaying colonial houses.

The motorcycle bounced up and down the hills Diamante was famous for, often alongside terrifying cliffs. As they made their way down to the bay, Detective Alu could see the brilliant blue of the Atlantic Ocean lazily embracing a tired shore.

Finally they reached the muddy
roads of the bay,
the newest part of the city.

The okada stopped suddenly, jerking the detective out of his thoughts.

The driver turned around
with a glint in his eye,
a little too content with the knowledge
that despite the detective's protests and insults,
they had arrived safely.

"You okay, sir?" he asked.
Detective Alu held his anger and thrust cash into the young man's hand.

With a grunt and a whir,
the okada—seemingly at wit's end—
was off, leaving only a puff of smoke and a dubious trail.

Detective Alu's dark face
was covered with a thin layer of sweat
that did nothing to veil his anger.

Holding Demons in Small Jars

Detective Alu gazed around him.

The late morning graced his cheek with a soft breeze
as the sun shone quietly, not yet beating down on the
poor residents of Diamante.

Though the crime scene was still a street away,
Alu could feel the weight of it,
the heaviness.

The kind that came before a Diamante rainfall.

The kind that betrayed an otherwise normal day in Diamante.

Today the air was tinged with the memory of lost lives.

To his right a group of women sat,
trading swears and compliments on the side of the street.
Their market stands burst with the weight of their
fruits and vegetables, an explosion of greens, reds and
yellows.

Jasmine Kumalah

As he ambled closer, they cooed at him in tones different
from the sharp insults they had spoken among themselves.

A young woman, more forceful then the others,
Made the move toward him, balancing mangoes on a tray.

He noticed that her left arm ended abruptly at her elbow.
It moved the air, a broken promise,
jagged and final in its end.
It was the sort of scar *the troubles* had left.

She noticed his eyes hovering
at the missing limb
and shifted her weight,
sheltering her arm from his gaze.

She instead drew his attention back to the tray of fruit
she balanced with one hand.

"You want sweet mango," she said, in a voice too sultry for
a woman selling mangoes.

He noticed the way in which she jutted her hips toward him
and the sliver of skin
peeking from her hastily wrapped lappa.

He guessed at what she might really be selling.

He grabbed a mango
and slipped her some coins,
leaving her with hips thrusting,
And lips pouting.

He heard the other women suck their teeth in despair.
They had missed a sale.

As he walked away, he heard their
chatter begin anew.
Now their insults were directed at the one-armed girl with
the sultry voice.

Chapter Two

The streets to the bay where the bodies were found were a maze.

Women clutched children between their legs
and men in the midst of curse-filled rants
navigated this waiting room of life.

Waiting
for death or
something else.

Maybe hope, the hope they had given up to live in this stifling oven.

Those who stayed too long lost their minds,

Holding Demons in Small Jars

or something else.
Something even more hidden.

He could see it,
their bodies taut
with unfulfilled promise.

Chapter Three

Detective Alu reached the dump by the bay
where the bodies had been found.
A steaming heap of refuse piled high,
it was the crowning jewel of the bay.

The stench hit him,
twisting itself before settling within his nostrils.

In the distance he saw Chief Bergain's
unmistakable figure. The large man and two others leaned
forward then backward, their eyes fixated on a spot in the
ground.

A group of locals
looked upon the scene,
seemingly bored by it all.

Alu knew, the gift of nonchalance
was one of the gifts *the troubles* had bestowed on the people.

Detective Alu smelled it first,
the stench of rotting flesh
beneath a burned surface.

But it was the sight of the bodies, their charred remains,
that transported him to another time,
unlocking a carefully guarded memory.

Grief swept across him,
straining his breath.

The humid air left him gasping.

He stilled his mind,
pressing the memory back down,
and focused on the scene in front of him.

To the now,
to the this,
to the here.

It was in this moment that Bergain looked up, an expression of relief on his face.

"Finally, Detective Alu. Where have you been?"

Detective Alu still felt the strain of withholding buried memory. But somehow his lips squeezed out an excuse about bad roads and cocky drivers.

Chapter Four

The troubles had
left the country reeling
and struggling to rebuild.

The Diamante police department
was left with
a stressed force
severely diminished
and underfunded.

UN Peacekeepers had been in charge of
police duties till the Bantunians could get back on their feet.

Now the Peacekeepers were gone.

Holding Demons in Small Jars

Alu knew Bergain needed a man like him more than anything.

Alu was a man with an eye for detail
and a unique ability to uncover stories others couldn't,
a man who could read the clues
no one else could.

After all, all they had were bodies
and stories to uncover.

Chapter Five

As Detective Alu kneeled to view the bodies better, Bergain brought him up to speed.

An international humanitarian group had caught wind of what had happened. They had started a campaign asking for justice to be brought. With international funding on the line the local government had to act.

"The Minister of Justice wants us to prosecute someone—immediately," Bergain said.

At the mention of the Minister of Justice, Detective Alu's concentration was broken.

Bergain nodded. "This is government business now, it looks bad for tourism. 'Barbaric' Africans do not sell."

The political machine was already at work. As always Detective Alu knew that nothing it did would be in service of these boys, brutally killed.

The Minister of Justice didn't care about these war boys. They had been useful during *the troubles*, but now the war was over. Everyone knew it wasn't only the rebels who used boy soldiers. In the midst of the war the desperate government turned its eye away from the colonels who recruited young boys in the name of saving the country.

The government had made a big deal about giving the boys jobs. They had given those war boys okadas.

"We will reteach them,
we will rehabilitate them," they had said.

They had used all kinds of big words in the shadow of the Western powers,
words they started to believe.

They laughed,
shook hands,
and spoke of a new Bantunia, a better Bantunia.

But what of the boys? They were still dying.

Chapter Six

The details surrounding the deaths of the three bay boys were scant,
lost in the mouths of closed-lipped residents.

To learn that story, Detective Alu knew he must bide his time.

In Diamante one became accustomed to waiting.

People waited for the lights to come back.
Waited for the generators' hum to cover the city.
Waited in the congested streets.
Waited for the roads to be fixed.
Waited for the politicians' promises to finally come true.

Waiting was braided through every action everyone took in Diamante.

Detective Alu didn't mind all the waiting.

The other police officers nicknamed him Ghost.
Detective Alu had a way of making himself part of a place, unnoticed but ever-present.

He had a way of moving without leaving a trace.
In a world where silences coated truths, Detective Alu had learned that solving mysteries required the sort of patience he had long cultivated.

Like everything in Diamante, in time, the story had a way of unraveling, like the thread of a tailor.

He need only wait.

Chapter Seven

For the next two weeks, Detective Alu came to the bay every day.

At first it seemed
the bay had swallowed the stories of
the three charred bodies and left nothing but quiet bones.

A
loyal
silence
hung over the bay,
refusing to speak about the events that transpired.

On some days he sat down with the old grandmother selling pepper mangoes.

When she heard his voice, she called out for him to sit by her, said he reminded her of her sons.

She claimed to be one hundred and ten, but he suspected she was only eighty. People in the days of her birth often used a major climate event to mark the year. With memory, the age of people often got muddled. She had been born the day after a great flood had swept through her village. As the river had swelled her mother had begun going into labor.

She had been born with feet wet she told him. The river had birthed her.

These days she was almost blind but she could still catch the hand of a thief and sniff false money from a distance.

Her eyes had a slight glaze over them, like the mist of Bantunia's mountains.

She had come from up-country during *the troubles*.
Her husband and three sons had been killed.

Now she lived with her daughters and their families.

She sold the mangoes to help out.

She dreamed of her village up there in the mountains.
She dreamed of going back there.

But as the years passed, she was contented that one day the river would call her back.

Jasmine Kumalah

Detective Alu would sit back in these moments, listening to her tell tales of bush witches and carnivorous spirits living deep in the mountains.

On other days he sat down with old man Tam, listening to tales of heroes long dead.

Tam had been a child when the British left.
His parents had taken him to the independence parade.
He had worn black shoes, a new pair his father bought with his soldier's small salary. How proud he had been that day, wearing his first pair of black shoes.

Tam had always lived by the bay.
His family had been here long before *the troubles*,
now the bay was filled with the people from up-country.
Even when *the troubles* ended, none of the people returned to their homes.

Instead the community gripping the bay simply grew, feeding itself.

On occasion Detective Alu walked with the sultry-voiced mango seller he now knew as Eliz.

When they took her arm she hadn't cried out. That is all she remembered.

She was a child then.

Her mother had lost both arms.
Her mother stayed home and Eliz went out to sell.

He never asked about the men at night.
And she never spoke of it.

Holding Demons in Small Jars

On this particular day he simply watched a group
of young boys playing football with
an old metal can, transforming it with every kick into the
contours of a ball.

They had all been born after *the troubles* but he wondered
to himself if they too carried the weight of *the troubles* they
had never known.

Chapter Eight

As Detective Alu made himself part of this place, as he tied himself to their daily activities, truth wafted forth.

Those whose mouths were not screwed shut found occasion to let the wind carry their voices toward the waiting ears of Detective Alu.

Eliz whispered to him one morning
that Masula was the man to talk to.

He could be found at the bar every night
clinging to his favorite drink,
the sweet wine of the native palm. Small wooden benches
were the outdoor bar's only décor
and the sounds of the latest Diamante rapper
served as the backdrop.

Holding Demons in Small Jars

With the smell of palm wine heavy on his breath,
Masula steadied himself on the bench beside Detective Alu.

"You are that detective man,"
Masula said in his staggering speech.

Detective Alu strained to decipher his words and nodded.

"I know everything," Masula muttered.

Detective Alu knew that Masula would need no prodding.
He knew from his work that people had a need to talk;
that too many people held the small horrors of their lives
close to their hearts; that too often people had a habit of
holding demons in small jars. But eventually those demons
needed to be let out. They always needed to speak.
On this night, Masula the drunkard had a demon to release
and Detective Alu sat waiting to hear.

With the sounds
of hip-hop in the background
And the occasional sip of palm wine on the part of Masula,

the story of the three boys began to be told.

There were three of them.
They were not right in the mind since the troubles, *you know.*

Too many of those children came out not right in the head.

They remember stuff they did.
We remember stuff they did.

So they come back crazy
and nobody wants them.

Jasmine Kumalah

*Those kids, nobody wanted them
so they went crazy.*

*Always fighting,
Stealing.*

Nobody wanted them.

But you know me, I feel sorry for them a bit.

I give them work.

*I'm a carpenter,
I fix things,
make things.*

*I have no sons.
My wife, her womb is no good.*

*During the troubles they beat her badly
and now the doctor says no more children.*

*I had a son but he died before the troubles.
He was sick, always sick.*

*We took him to the witch doctor
who gave him a potion,
but he died.*

*Witches are strong,
stronger than witch doctors sometimes.*

*So I take these kids like my own,
I take them under my wing.*

Holding Demons in Small Jars

I tell them to stop fighting,
to take a hammer
and to put
hurt
and
anger there.

The older two are
really crazy in the head.

It's no good,
too much death in there,
not enough life.

They don't know how to live any more.

But the younger one,
he listens, he hears me.

He comes back to me.
He says he wants to learn,
so I teach him, you know,
and he is good.

This boy he is good.
But the older boys,
they always come for him.

They are family now
so he goes with them.

But I tell him stay, stay with me.
Learn to be a carpenter.

Jasmine Kumalah

He says they are his brothers.
They have spilled the same blood together.

He tells me he will convince them
to come back,
to work with me.

But he never came back
and
now
he's dead.
Dead with them,
his brothers.

Chapter Nine

Detective Alu went to the home of
Baitra Fellons.

A man whose power
in the bay
was the invisible thread
that kept
the bay moving toward an uncertain future.

He was the man who collected
the rent
and
the man who oversaw
things when the police force couldn't.

Jasmine Kumalah

Sad thing, that business of the boys, Detective Alu.
I don't know what gets into our people some days.
We become what the British like to call us,
primitive, primal, beastly.
We do unheard of things.

You remember the troubles, *Detective.*
The things that happened.
Yes,
these things. We are capable of them, Detective.
Sometimes it boils in the people's blood.

Sad business, this thing of the boys,
but people must protect themselves, Detective.
Against threat,
against
filth.
Filth.
These wayward boys are the plague of our country.
We must rid our society of them.
If we want to rebuild,
they cannot continue to terrorize us.

And what do you people, the police, do,
in your offices?
You do not come to protect us here in the bay from the filth
that threatens to cover us.
So, yes, perhaps the people tire of it and take matters into their
own hands.
But
what else can we do?
We cannot wait.
We waited once
and what became of us?

No, we take things into our own hands here in the bay.
We do not tolerate
filth, we do not.
This business of the boys is sad, but it is necessary, Detective, it is necessary.

Alu sighed. The war had given birth to a particularly violent form of justice, one directed by shapeless mobs.

He heard stories of people beaten by mobs due to alleged stealing.

They were beaten till their blood mingled with the earth.

Leave it be, the halls of authority whispered.

Leave it be. Let them enact their own form of justice.

So we have done it, Alu thought. We the police have let it be and now a new sort of horror has been born.

Chapter Ten

The boys were buried
on a day much like the day
his dear wife was buried.

It was the most treacherous of mercies that left a man alive
when the rest of his family was dead.

Unscathed while those he loved lay buried.

This
is
what
the
neighbors

Holding Demons in Small Jars

told him:
They, the rebels, made her dance
As they paraded her mother
then her father naked.
Then they shot them
and told her to keep dancing.

They, the rebels,
locked her

in the house.

The house on the hill they had saved up for,
with the sea hovering in the distance.

A home
finally,
to grow
to love
to make love
to give love.

She was finally pregnant.
They had been trying for so long.

A girl, he hoped.

A girl with her smile
and deep brown eyes.
The eyes that
pleaded for him to stay
whenever he was called to go protect the inner city.

Jasmine Kumalah

The rebels,
only young boys,
set the house on fire.

They watched her burn.
Intoxicated by their own acts of violence.
Dancing in the streets
shooting bullets
from bloodied guns.

As she screamed to be saved,
she had pleaded for the baby inside of her,
she had pleaded for him to save her.

And
he
had
not
come.

They,
the neighbors,
stopped watching then.

They were sorry.

That day.
He came running back.

He heard that
the rebels had
made it up the hill.

Holding Demons in Small Jars

Their hill.
His hill.

Her parents,
they had left their home in the north, up-country.
You will be safe with us, he had said.
Come to us, he had said.

That morning, he hadn't wanted to leave.
But he was needed,
so he went.

She let him go.
He let her go.

He found the home,
the charred remains of it.
He found
the bodies of his in-laws.
And he found her,
frozen in her
agony.

The neighbors pulled him away screaming
and kicking.

Broken.

They pulled him away before
the rebels came again. That night he and the others hid in a church. The next day he returned to his house. His neighbors silently helped him bury the bodies of his love and her parents.

Jasmine Kumalah

Not a night passed since that day that Detective Alu did not wake with the dreams of
young boys whose eyes danced with flickers of flames.

They all held demons within.
They all did.

Chapter Eleven

It was Eliz who finally told him the story, the whole story.

One of her night visitors had told her how it all happened.

We, some men from the bay, were playing cards,
chewing kola, drinking palm wine.

It was a normal day.

The boys had shown up but no one had paid any mind to them.

They were the dung flies
hovering at the edge,
their eyes red
with the smoke of cannabis,
barely holding onto today's reality.

Jasmine Kumalah

*So the men kept
playing cards, drinking palm wine, chewing their kola and paying
no mind to the boys.*

*But then a man came running from down the way.
He yelled for the men to catch the boys.*

*A woman
was yelling at the top of her lungs,
a
long
chilling
wail.*

"They have robbed me,
they have robbed me,
those boys,
those demons,
they have robbed me."

Two men sitting on the corner sprang up
and caught the boys before they could run.

Now that he thought about it, the boys had looked confused,
as confused as the men.

They had not run.

By then other men stopped playing and started gathering.

They dragged the boys down to the woman and she confirmed
that it was them.

Holding Demons in Small Jars

She was the Fellons woman.
Sister of Baitra Fellons, the big man in the bay.

The Fellons woman was not right in the head, so one person said
maybe she was wrong.

But another woman, the one who lived across from the Fellons
woman, said she too had seen the youngest boy walking out
of the Fellons woman's house.

The boys protested their innocence,
but how were people to believe them?
The boys were thieves, they always had been.

We must make them an example, they had agreed.

They stripped the boys of their clothes,
and walked them through the bay.
A warning to anyone else.

People cheered.
They felt like heroes.

Rocks
bounced
off the boys' flesh.

The smaller boys of the bay took sticks,
hitting the thieves as they walked.

The boys pleaded now, the man who told Eliz remembered.
We are innocent of this crime, they said.
We do not steal, they said.
We are heading up to Masula, they said.
We are not the thieves, they said.

Jasmine Kumalah

This is what they had said.

But the boys were thieves,
and thieves were liars, everyone agreed.
And the Fellons woman was not right in the head
but even she could tell a thief, they all agreed.

One of the older men
said we can't have these criminals on the loose
doing the devil's work.

He was a converted Baptist.
He went to church every Sunday.

Demons walk in man's skin,
he declared.

Look at their eyes, he said,
Demons have eyes that shine red.

One of the men swore he saw the blaze of red in their eyes
and the men,
they were scared
and they beat the boys harder.

Beat the demon in them,
they had to beat the demon in them.

Then one,
one of the boys fell to the ground,
moving
like a snake.

Who was it who yelled for them to be burned?
The man did not remember.

Holding Demons in Small Jars

But before he knew it, they had all agreed.

The filth had to burn.
The demons had to burn.

Kerosene,
found in the nearby bar.

Matches,
grabbed from one of the men.

The boys
pleaded, now that he remembered.

But thieves lie, everyone knows that.

He can't remember who threw the kerosene on them.
He can't remember who threw the match.

The boys screeched like demons
as they burned in hell's fire.

We watched them burn, the man said,
the demons,
those boys,
we watched them burn.

The man,
the one who was Baptist-saved
turned to them.

We have done the work of God,
he said.

Jasmine Kumalah

They went back home,
The smell of burned flesh on their brows.

They drank palm wine heavily that night, they chewed on kola
nuts, they lost more than usual at their cards
and they waited,
for what they did not know.

Perhaps deliverance,
for they no longer knew whose sin was greater.

Eliz's man had not wanted sex that night.
He had only wanted to be held
as he sobbed.

Sorry for himself
and the boys he had helped kill that day.

Eliz simply held him.

Chapter Twelve

When *the troubles* ended
the people of Diamante
had reached out
for a normalcy
they no longer knew.

Mothers who had buried daughters,
sons who had killed fathers,
reached out for a normalcy
they had long forgotten.

But *the troubles*
had buried its demons
within their hearts,
They twisted themselves in each person's
gut,
springing out
on occasion from
the bellies of despair.

Those
who had enacted revenge

Jasmine Kumalah

on the boys
were as nameless
and shapeless
as the charred bodies that had stared up at Alu.

Somewhere,
somehow,
something
had broken, and none of them knew how to fix it.

Chapter Thirteen

The order came from Bergain Maxine.
The case had grown stale.
In these tropical climates,
things festered and rotted quickly.

The shelf life of life was low.

Let it be,
Alu was told.

Chapter Fourteen

From Masula, he learned that the boys
called each other
Rahmi
Abou
and
Sira

They had names.
Once they had family.

He walked to the place in the bay, where their bodies had
been buried,
unclaimed and unmarked
under gray concrete.

Holding Demons in Small Jars

He took his pocketknife
and engraved their names
on the slabs.

He was not a praying man
but today he prayed that death
gave them the peace
that life had never given them.

Finally.

Acknowledgements

I would like to express my gratitude to the many people who saw me through this book; to all those who provided support, talked things over, read, wrote, offered comments, assisted in the editing, proofreading and design.

I would like to thank my writing mentor Nora Esthimer for believing in my words and for all her help in making this book move from dream to reality.

I would like to thank my good friend and illustrator Si Jie Loo for gifting her beautiful visual language to this story.

Above all I want to thank my parents Lans Kumalah and Forster Kumalah and sisters Jerrie Kumalah and Sayon Robinson, who have always supported me in my writing and other endeavors.

I would also like to thank my chosen family, my dear friends who at different parts of the journey have read and supported my work.

And lastly I will like to thank my copy editor and book designer for crafting my story into a format I can share.

Jasmine Kumalah

Jasmine Kumalah is a Belgian born, Sierra Leonean and Togolese- American writer. She writes stories, poetry and pursues other creative endeavors. This is her first published work.

Si Jie Loo is a Malaysian born artist living and working in Santa Barbara.

Made in the USA
Lexington, KY
28 June 2016